IN A U-HAUL NORTH OF DAMASCUS

BOOKS BY DAVID BOTTOMS

In a U-Haul North of Damascus   1983
Shooting Rats at the Bibb County Dump   1980
Jamming With the Band at the VFW (chapbook)   1978

In a U-Haul
North of
Damascus

David Bottoms

WILLIAM MORROW AND COMPANY, INC.

New York   1983

Though sometimes in different versions, the poems in this collection originally appeared in the pages of these magazines: *American Poetry Review, Atlanta Magazine, Atlantic Monthly, Black Warrior Review, Crazy Horse, Iowa Review, Missouri Review, The New Yorker, Paris Review, Ploughshares, Poetry, Quarterly West,* and *The Virginia Quarterly Review.*

"The Copperhead," which appeared in a slightly different version in *Shooting Rats at the Bibb County Dump,* was first published in *Atlantic Monthly.*

"Under the Boathouse," was first published in *The New Yorker,* copyright © 1982.

"In a U-Haul North of Damascus," "Rest at the Mercy House," "A Home Buyer Watches the Moon," "Hurricane," "In the Wilderness Motel," "In the Black Camaro," "Rendezvous: Belle Glade," "Wakulla: Chasing the Gator's Eye," "The Drowned," and "The Boy Shepherds' Simile" originally appeared in *Poetry,* copyright © 1981 and 1982 by the Modern Poetry Association.

"The Fox" appeared in the *Antioch Review.*

Thanks to the Florida State University for two university fellowships which provided the time to write these poems.

Special thanks to Maria Carvainis, Maria Guarnaschelli, and Van K. Brock.

Library of Congress Cataloging in Publication Data

Bottoms, David.
In a u-haul north of Damascus.

I. Title.
PS3552.O819I5   1983   811'.54   82-22938
ISBN 0-688-02067-4
ISBN 0-688-01743-6 (pbk.)

Printed in the United States of America

First Edition

1 2 3 4 5 6 7 8 9 10

BOOK DESIGN BY MARIA EPES

for Lynn

CONTENTS

I

II

III

IV

V

It is hard sometimes to remember that beauty is another word for reality.
——ROBERT PENN WARREN

Sickness is not only in body, but in that part we used to call: soul.
——MALCOLM LOWRY

REST AT THE MERCY HOUSE

Because nature doesn't specialize
in mercy, this House of Refuge was raised behind the dunes
on Gilbert's Bar,
provisioned with fuel and blankets, cereals
and dried meat, for the survivors of ships wrecked
on offshore reefs. And in its time
adequate to its vision.

Now with others
we parade behind the hatchery and marvel
how the newborn turtles cobble the bottom of their tank,
wander past aquariums of native fish,
tap our fingers against the glass, little codes
we want them to know us by, then tread
the boardwalk down to the beach
where survivors in another time waded
toward shore with whatever they could salvage,
mostly themselves.
                    No more shipwrecks
off this coast, only a few survivors of wrecked
or uncharted lives, a few tourists
looking for a place to beach. Across the dunes
the sea oats wash back and forth in a gold froth;
gulls and black skimmers, pelicans and terns,
take sanctuary in the weathered hollows of the sea wall.
Here nothing is molested, all blest.
For travelers like us, a tour of the house, a vision,
a momentary rest.

HIKING TOWARD LAUGHING GULL POINT

Once I saw a gull catch a bait in midair.
Climbing until the slack ran out,
it snapped back like a white feather on the end of a whip
and fell into the sea.

We've all swallowed a line or two,
a real estate deal, some bad investment of faith, or so
I tell myself as I walk
past the fishermen casting their cut shrimp on the water,
the overweight women wading in the surf,
the tower where the boy lifeguard hangs against the blue sky
and dreams behind his sunglasses a dream of salvation.

As I near the same sandy point I hike toward every year,
stand at the edge of the wing-
flutter, my white skin burning red, the sun bleaching
what's left of my hair, I think how the point
keeps drifting farther away
like some water-mirage
or a piece of land in a speculator's dream.
How each summer I search for my dream
vacation, only to find myself feeling more like some gull
climbing toward the edge of an island,
a hook, the end of the line.

NEIGHBORS, THROWING KNIVES

In the woods at the corner of our yards
we hang the plywood squares,
the Magic Marker images of pronghorn, panther,
grizzly, whitetail,
and step off the paces we use to measure
our skill.
               Here in the soft light filtering
through needles and cones, green shifting
membrane of poplar, hickory, live oak,
white skin of dogwood beginning
to flower, we heft the blades,
grind points on stone, gauge the fine balance
between what is real and what is imagined,
the knives bringing all the animals to life
and killing them again
as our throws bury steel deep in the heart
of the quivering wood and the blades tremble
back through their bones.
                      In our own hearts
we love what they might be, their shapes
frozen in brush as though, suddenly,
they had turned from wood
and caught our scent drifting in a wind-shift.
So we hunt this suburb, whet our aim
to move among them in the little wilderness
beyond the bricked-in beds of azaleas,
sunflowers tied against tall sticks,
the half-acres of razored grass,
trellised vines, boxwoods manicured by wives.

The whole neighborhood is quiet.
The architect who lives across the street
is now the architect of dreams, his cedar split-level
still as a crypt on the landscaped hill.
In the brick ranch house
the city planner turns another spadeful of dirt,
a groundbreaking for his own monument. And I,
who can no longer afford to live
in my two-story, have come out into the street
to stare past the mailboxes at an abrupt dead end.

Quietly now the bats jerk
in and out of the streetlight, their shadows
zipping across the grass like black snakes.
And the moon lies balanced on the roof of my house
like a new gold coin, or the simple face
of an angel in a colonial cemetery.

LOCAL QUARRELS

As though the nineteenth century hadn't crumbled
and polite society still made pretensions
about honor, we left the party boozing in the house,
and half walking, half staggering,
followed our principals across the backyard
and gas-lamped garden,
the barbwire fence, the pasture spotted with ponds.

All around us oak branches trembled,
and far across the field of ponds and black mounds
of cattle sleeping in clusters in the cool dew,
we could see against a dark horizon of pines
the light that was the house.

Face to face they stood in the full-moonlight
surrounding them with shadows,
arms at their sides, and began on signal
to step in opposite directions, looking straight ahead
as we all counted with our hearts
the twelve quick paces before they turned
and the long pistol-cracks spread through the pasture.
Heads cocked in sudden amazement,
they listened as the shots faded and one cow lowed
and waded into water. When neither fell
they sat in a common shadow.

FOG ON KENNESAW

We pitch our tent on Kennesaw Mountain,
pull the hemp rope tight, set the steel stakes,
lean our pick and shovels against the trees
like the rifles of Joe Johnson's army.
On the south side of the mountain,
we are hidden from the park rangers, clothed
in the brush like the ghosts of Loring's Rebels.

Nothing has changed here but the century.
These same neutral stars
saw Rebels shoot rocks from cannons.
Trees along these slopes and fields hold rifle balls
in their healed-over bark.
                        At sunrise
we will patrol Little Kennesaw for minié balls and bayonets,
scour the woods where McPherson drove his Yankees
into the eyeballs of French's cannons. But tonight
we have found something seeping up through the leaf-cover,
the pine straw, something drifting across old earthworks,
maneuvering on Kennesaw.

RECORDING THE SPIRIT VOICES

In the hollow below the hill vaults
I have placed a recorder
on the grave of a young woman killed in a fire
and have crouched under the arm of this angel
to wait for voices,
tree frogs whirring through the blue pines,
the Ocmulgee lapping the bank at the foot of Rose Hill.

A gray moon over the Confederate graves
gleams on the water,
the white gallon jugs floating some man's trotline.
Like me, he's trying to bring things to the surface
where they don't belong.

And across the river
blue needles rasp like the voices
I heard on television,
the documented whisper of spirits, *I'm afraid here, I'm afraid.*
So am I now
as leaves in the hollow rustle their dry tongues:
afraid to hear a woman scream from a burning house,
to record some evidence her tombstone lied,
bury the truth these angels stand on: *born* and *died.*

THE TENT ASTRONOMER

As a barrier against mosquitoes,
I pull an old sheet from the closet,
then cross the yard,
enter the field bordering the orange grove
where the sleeping bag lies behind the low tripod,
the hammer and stakes wait in the damp grass.

At each corner
one stake goes into the sandy ground,
then the sheet stretched over the four points,
pulled down and anchored with stones.
The darkness underneath is private.

I lie still for a while
and listen to cicadas crying by the canal,
the crickets and barking toads,
stinkbugs breaking against the walls like small clods,
then with my knife
cut a hole for the barrel,
let lens and mirror lift me up toward light.

TURNING THE DOUBLE PLAY
for Doug Fowler

In the noon-swelter, dust
hanging over the infield like red fog, we stand at the edge
of the grass and watch the ball draw white arcs
toward home, the umpire easing back on his heels,
a coach behind the backstop
second-guessing.

In the oak shade behind third base, our wives
sit in lawn chairs and guard our cooler of Gatorade.
They wonder why we never win,
and why we seem content to stand out here at the edge
of middle age and watch the hits line into the outfield.
They say, *the teams you play are so young.*

Yes, they are. And some runner's always on first,
the heat rising in waves off the cracked dirt, the bat
a blur and a white shot toward short. And even
when the double play is finally turned, the way we both
turned it years ago on different teams in different leagues,
nothing is won back for more than a moment.

SIGN FOR MY FATHER,
WHO STRESSED THE BUNT

On the rough diamond,
the hand-cut field below the dog lot and barn,
we rehearsed the strict technique
of bunting. I watched from the infield,
the mound, the backstop
as your left hand climbed the bat, your legs
and shoulders squared toward the pitcher.
You could drop it like a seed
down either base line. I admired your style,
but not enough to take my eyes off the bank
that served as our center-field fence.

Years passed, three leagues of organized ball,
no few lives. I could homer
into the garden beyond the bank,
into the left-field lot of Carmichael Motors,
and still you stressed the same technique,
the crouch and spring, the lead arm absorbing
just enough impact. That whole tiresome pitch
about basics never changing,
and I never learned what you were laying down.

Like a hand brushed across the bill of a cap,
let this be the sign
I'm getting a grip on the sacrifice.

THE BOY SHEPHERDS' SIMILE

Wind rose cold under our robes, and straw blew loose
from the stable roof.
We loved the cow tied to the oak, her breath rising
in the black air, and the two goats trucked
from the Snelling farm, the gray dog shaking with age
and weather.
                  Over our scene a great star hung
its light, and we could see in the bleached night
a crowd of overcoats peopling the chairs.
A coat of black ice glazed the street.

This was not a child or a king,
but Mary Sosebee's Christmas doll of a year ago.
We knelt in that knowledge on the wide front lawn
of the First Baptist Church
while flashbulbs went off all around us
and a choir of angels caroled from their risers.
This was not a child wrapped in the straw
and the ragged sheet, but since believing was an easy thing
we believed it was like a child,
a king who lived in the stories we were told.
For this we shivered in adoration. We bore the cold.

SERMON OF THE FALLEN

From an east window
a screen of light sliced across the walnut box.
I sat and watched the grain rise dark,
and listened to him tell
how muscles wither under the skin
and the skin dries and flakes away from the bone
like gray bark flaking from the trunk of a fallen pine,
how the forest trembles only once as the tree falls
and somewhere a bird whimpers from a ridge,
then nothing,
and what needles are left yellow-green
and clinging to limbs
shimmer only a few more times in the rain, then lose
all color and drop away,
and the gray pine shines through the bark like bone,
cracks and sours, softens with larva,
collapses in shadow, belches gas
from its grainy soup, dries
in sun to a black forest dust, then seeps
with one last rain through the pine-needle floor
and becomes earth. So, he said, you had come to fall.
Even as a boy, I could feel the trembling in us all.

II

RENDEZVOUS: BELLE GLADE

Pine thicket at the edge of a clearing:
I squatted with my back against a tree
and cradled in my lap the Enfield carbine,
a pawnshop gun, not terribly accurate,
but terrible and accurate enough,
a jungle weapon designed for use in Burma.
Under black branches I knew were green
as money, I hefted its weight,
checked night vision through peep sight
and saw over the dull gleam
of the cone-shaped flash suppressor
the field where Florida sand boiled up
like smoke and fireflies snapped off
against the far border of trees.
Inside those trees a truck sat under a canopy
of low branches, and around that canopy
Cubans hid and listened for a voice
on the two-way radio.
                    I listened for an owl
to call again from the pines dissolving
into glades behind me, for the voices
of tree frogs to blur toward a monkey-laugh
riddling the trees of Burma, for wind
to crackle like brush under boots,
and felt in my heart a weakness like malaria,
which I knew was only the shaking
of nerves, like the tips of my fingers
caressing the scars on the Enfield,
tracing crude letters of the one deep scar
that was the name the soldier Lowry
had carved into his stock.
                    From the sky
came the first sign, a far-off, insect drone

of an engine buzzing the dark above
the southern horizon, then a burst of light
stringing the edges of the field
and the airstrip glowing in the forest
like a flesh wound. I found my hands close
around the rifle as the droning grew loud
and twin props swept tree-level and were gone,
leaving only a wake in the pinetops
and a blown field of wrapped bales hitting
between the strands of light
and rolling in the sand like paratroops.
In the darkness of snuffed lanterns,
I stood in a silence awaiting all-clear,
wondered what I might do if a floodlight
of the law should jar from the trees.
I tapped the magazine, thought of Lowry
killed and buried in Burma,
or alive, perhaps, with family in England,
his retirement and his life closing in,
and how on other nights
he sat listening in a jungle for Japs,
how silence made him as jumpy as noise
and nerves edged a name in his stock.

LIGHT OF THE SACRED HARP

Small fire of hymnals in a trash can,
the spirit of shape-notes rising in smoke
as we huddle at the altar, watch
our song-cloud hover under the ceiling,
rise through a broken window
into the cold dark. Here we share
in the good new warmth of God's old house,
the warmth of the bottle carried through woods
and field. Here we drink the new wine,
the plasma of visionaries and hunters,
until the spirit of that blood moves
in us, moves in the legs
of the offering table, the swayed backs
of pews, the splintered crosses bearing panes
of wavy glass, dark faces frowning
from the table of the Last Supper, staring
through the ashes of our hymn-words
floating up like dust on fire, floating up
and vanishing like the yelps of our dogs
vanishing in the trees beyond the field
of stumps, the tombstones
weedy with briars, the collapsed steps,
the jimmied door.
                    As though this were a light
to see all things by, the fire draws us
into its vision, a choir of voices rising
behind the crackling music, a clapping
of sweaty hands, swaying of bodies
in a hot night, the slap of rhythm sticks,
tambourines, bottle caps rattling
in a hollow gourd. And we chunk in hymnals,
funeral home fans of the Sermon on the Mount,
Jesus in the wilderness, Jesus at the door,

chunk in a bouquet of dead flowers
to watch the fire jump around the pulpit
like something catching spirit, hear
old voices burning back from the graveyard
in new-found harmony as the pulpit catches
and becomes light, and we kneel
for drunkness and joy as fire climbs the wall
and enters the Last Supper, the air filling up
with psalm-smoke, the whole house of the Lord
popping with revival, becoming pure spirit
of voices returning in the joyful noise
of the Sacred Harp, singing over and over
the good gospel news that men do rise from dust
and ashes.

IN THE BLACK CAMARO

Through the orange glow of taillights,
I crossed the dirt road, entered
the half-mile of darkness and owl screech,
tangled briar and fallen trunk, followed
the yellow beam of Billy Parker's flashlight
down the slick needle-hill,
half crawling, half sliding and kicking
for footholds, tearing up whole handfuls
of scrub brush and leaf mold
until I jumped the mud bank, walked
the ankle-deep creek,
the last patch of pine, the gully,
and knelt at the highway stretching
in front of Billy Parker's house,
spotted the black Chevy Camaro parked
under a maple not fifty feet
from the window where Billy Parker rocked
in and out of view,
studying in the bad light of a table lamp
the fine print of his Allstate policy.
I cut the flashlight, checked up
and down the highway. Behind me
the screech growing distant, fading
into woods, but coming on
a network of tree frogs signaling
along the creek. Only that, and the quiet
of my heels coming down on asphalt
as I crossed the two-lane and stood
at the weedy edge of Billy Parker's yard,
stood in the lamp glare of the living room
where plans were being made to make me rich
and thought of a boat and Johnson outboard,
of all the lures on a K-Mart wall,
of reels and graphite rods, coolers

of beer, weedy banks of dark fishy rivers,
and of Billy Parker rocking in his chair,
studying his coverage, his bank account,
his layoff at Lockheed, his wife laboring
in the maternity ward
of the Cobb General Hospital. For all
of this, I crouched in the shadow
of fender and maple, popped the door
on the Camaro, and found
in the faint house-light drifting
through the passenger's window
the stripped wires hanging below the dash.
I took the driver's seat, kicked
the clutch, then eased again
as I remembered the glove box
and the pint of Seagram's Billy Parker
had not broken the seal on. Like an alarm
the tree frogs went off in the woods.
I drank until they hushed
and I could hear through cricket chatter
the rockers on Billy Parker's chair
grinding ridges into his living room floor,
worry working on him like hard time.
Then a wind working in river grass,
a red current slicing
around stumps and river snags, a boat-drift
pulling against an anchor
as I swayed in the seat of the black Camaro,
grappled for the wires
hanging in darkness between my knees,
saw through the tinted windshield
by a sudden white moon
rolling out of the clouds, a riverbank
two counties away, a place to jump and roll
on the soft shoulder of the gravel road,
a truck in a thicket a half-mile downstream.

UNDER THE BOATHOUSE

Out of my clothes, I ran past the boathouse
to the edge of the dock
and stood before the naked silence of the lake,
on the drive behind me, my wife
rattling keys, calling for help with the grill,
the groceries wedged into the trunk.
Near the tail end of her voice, I sprang
from the homemade board, bent body
like a hinge, and speared the surface,
cut through water I would not open my eyes in,
to hear the junked depth pop in both ears
as my right hand dug into silt and mud,
my left clawed around a pain.
In a fog of rust I opened my eyes to see
what had me, and couldn't, but knew
the fire in my hand and the weight of the thing
holding me under, knew the shock of all
things caught by the unknown
as I kicked off the bottom like a frog,
my limbs doing fearfully strange strokes,
lungs collapsed in a confusion of bubbles,
all air rising back to its element.
I flailed after it, rose toward the bubbles
breaking on light, then felt down my arm
a tug running from a taut line.
Halfway between the bottom of the lake
and the bottom of the sky, I hung like a buoy
on a short rope, an effigy
flown in an underwater parade,
and imagined myself hanging there forever,
a curiosity among fishes, a bait hanging up
instead of down. In the lung-ache,
in the loud pulsing of temples, what gave first
was something in my head, a burst

of colors like the blind see, and I saw
against the surface a shadow like an angel
quivering in a dead-man's float,
then a shower of plastic knives and forks
spilling past me in the lightened water, a can
of barbequed beans, a bottle of A.1., napkins
drifting down like white leaves,
heavenly litter from the world I struggled toward.
What gave then was something on the other end,
and my hand rose on its own and touched my face.
Into the splintered light under the boathouse,
the loved, suffocating air hovering over the lake,
the cry of my wife leaning dangerously
over the dock, empty grocery bags at her feet,
I bobbed with a hook through the palm of my hand.

III

THE CHRISTMAS RIFLE

Over the spine of the ridge
orange light scatters through pine and briar,
sifts into the gorge.
With the red glove of his right hand
my father points toward a branch near the top of a pine,
raises the sawed-off stock to my shoulder, lifts
the barrel and backs away.

The gray squirrel moves in front of the sun,
and light shoots down the barrel like a ricochet,
turns blued steel silver from bead to sight.
He points again
and I follow the dark green sleeve of his jacket
to his red outstretched finger
to the squirrel crouched in the fork where the branch
joins the trunk.

Don't jerk. Don't pull. And I watch that spot of air
where the gray squirrel jumps,
then drops from limb to limb in stiff gymnastics
until it strikes the ground at the foot of the pine.
I cradle the rifle and walk to the squirrel, prod
the soft belly with the barrel, study
the hole over the left shoulder, the fine gray hair,
white near the roots, puffed out around a circle of blood.
Just behind me, my father is walking on needles;
the weight of his hand comes down on my shoulder.

GIGGING ON ALLATOONA

Light bleeding onto pines
and pine shadows crawling across water turning orange
under boathouses floating under an orange sky,
we huddle on a ruined dock, file barbs sharp,
load buckets with ice and beer, wait
for the chorus of lake-edge croaking.

Darkness fallen, we shove off
onto the water, pull ourselves along the beams
our flashlights anchor to the bank
toward the bass-throb belching in the starless night,
the voice that dies as we drift toward a rustle
in the cove-grass, the cattails waving.
And when light finds the bulging slime eyes,
we feel the thrust and jab, the tilt
and rock, the small twitch of legs
kicking air at the end of the gig, the wake
rolling away from the boat far out across the black water.

THE COPPERHEAD

A dwarfed limb
or a fist-thick vine, he lay stretched
across a dead oak fallen into the water.
I saw him when I cast my lure
toward a cluster of stumps near the half-buried trunk,
then pulled the boat to the edge of the limbs.
One ripple ran up his back like the tail
of a wake,
and he lay still again, dark and patterned,
large on years of frogs and rats.

I worked the lure around the brush,
oak and poplar stumps rising out of the water
like the ruins of an old pier,
and watched his spade head shift on the dry bark.
But no bass struck
so I laid the rod across the floor of the boat,
sat for a long time watching the shadows
make him a part of the tree,
and wanted more than once to drift into the shaded water,
pull myself down a fallen branch toward the trunk
where he lay quiet and dangerous and unafraid,
all spine and nerve.

KINSHIP
for James Dickey

From the house on barrels, we cross
the floating dock, guide
long aluminum pipes into a finger of woods
toward the cove where moccasins sun on stones.

When pines open to swamp-cove and pads tread
toward deep water,
we stop and tuck our jeans into our boots,
draw wires from the handles of our guns,

through sun-glare skimming off the lake,
slosh toward the point of the cove,
move into an element neither earth nor water
but some dark blend, walking
or wading until we reach the island of rocks
and almost step on his tail. Startled,
the mouth flowers to a white bloom,
the black stem arches,
and we edge back toward the pines, after-fear
buzzing down our nerves.

Across the smooth rocks, we lie belly-down
in ridiculous postures,
lift the awkward tubes to our lips.
All of this to revive a venomous kinship
when the plane of air is slashed by the dart
and the last of the chambered breath
exits the blowgun with something like a hiss.

THE FOX

A quest brought a gray fox to the field behind my house.
In a circle of dirt
where drought had starved away the grass, he fell
to one knee, rubbed an ear on the ground
as though he were listening for heat to crack the field.

I snapped a clip into the handle of the Beretta
and stepped off the porch.

The slamming of the screen froze him. He stood up
and spread his legs for balance, shook a bright red halo
of dust around his head, and wandered toward me,
legs out of sync, mouth oozing saliva and mud.

He sidled along the edge of the field where tomato vines
fenced my yard, then struck a crooked path
between the stakes, tangled, and tripped to one shoulder.
The powdery soil rose around him like waves of heat.

I sat in a lawn chair and watched him wallow in exhaustion,
his dull, matted throat pulsing for quick breath.

Then nosing the air and the ground, the tomato leaves
and the dwarfed tomatoes, he caught a scent,
jerked his shoulders through vines and string,
staggered out of the tomato garden and into the yard

where what he needed to find moved in the blur
of the azalea bush and the guava tree, the lawn chair
and the long brown yard stretching toward the gray house.

THE DROWNED

Arms finned-out across the water,
he floated face down in the crotch of a fallen oak.
I cut the outboard
and rode the current, paddle-steered
toward the water stilled in the limbs of the tree.

In the bend where the river pooled and deepened,
my stomach jumped like something caught
and I pulled up short,
waited for breath, let my eyes follow water downstream
where the string of plastic milk jugs
floating my trotline
bobbed like heads on the surface of the river.

Then I drew the boat closer,
watched the slack of his blue jeans roll in my wake,
his head nod gently against the thick oak branch,
long hair tangled in the branch-twigs.
I eased the paddle out and touched his heel.
He didn't turn or move, only gazed straight down
into the deepest part of the Etowah
as though fascinated by something I couldn't see.

WAKULLA: CHASING THE GATOR'S EYE
for Steve Belew

If you catch a gleam between pad stalks
or a gleam among river trash bogged in the scum of algae,
cut the outboard and drift,
fix your spotlight on the eye's red shining.

Through the dark it will come to you
like a red reflector on the edge of a dock
where there is nothing like a dock,
only pads and algae, and the endless drift of the Wakulla
washing slowly under.
                          Ease toward it on that drift,
your light fixed on the eye's bright circle.
And if you approach as a part of this river, give over
to your truest self, something
washed down like all things washed toward the gulf,
the reflector will hold above the surface of the river,
and you will see in its deep, red shining
the reptile that moves beneath you.

IN A JON BOAT DURING A FLORIDA DAWN

Sunlight displaces stars
and on the Wakulla
long cypress shadows streak water burning
light and clear. If you look around you,
as you must, you see the bank dividing itself
into lights and darks, black waterbugs
stirring around algae beds, watermarks circling
gray trunks of cypress and oak,
a cypress knee fading under a darker moccasin,
silver tips of river grass breaking
through lighted water, silver backs of mullet
streaking waves of river grass.
For now, there are no real colors, only tones
promising change, a sense
of something developing, and no matter
how many times you have been here,
in this boat or another,
you feel an old surprise surfacing
in and around you. If you could,
you would cut the outboard
and stop it all right here at the gray height
of that anticipation. You would hide yourself
in this moment, cling to an oak branch
or a river snag
and stop even the slightest drift of the current.
In fresh sunlight distinguishing loggerhead
from stump, moss from stone,
you would give yourself completely
to the holding,
like the lizard clinging to the reed cover
or the red tick anchored in the pit of your knee.

DRUNKS IN THE BASS BOAT

One light across a mile of water, the porch-
light of the bait shop through layers
of pine. Along the far bank, the shadow
of the tree line floating and sinking
as moonlight sifts between cloud-gaps, casts
a long yellow rope across the lake. Beyond
the grass island cradling the boat, the pads
weeding back into the cove, a jungle
of lilies, white petaled heads curling
on long necks toward the water—
night herons.
              The outboard coughs and dies,
the cord jumps back into the casing,
and somewhere in the darkness off our bow,
a breaking of water, a stinkpot or frog
spooked into the shallows, a salamander
risking the bass cover. We pump the bulb,
check the gas line, the tank lying
under the cooler. Someone should have changed
the plug.
          All night we have trolled
the deep water, the banks, the weedy bottom
around the pads, thrown deep runners,
live shiners, plastic worms and lizards,
jigs and flies, a Vienna sausage, a sardine,
a wad of chewed gum, and for all our tackle
have failed again to dredge up the one dream
bass to swim forever above our bronzed names
on the trophy wall of the Lake Jackson bait shop,
or even a few good crappie for the iron pans
rusting on our kitchen walls.
            And now the motor
choked down in the pad stalks, stalled

in the quiet water needled with grass, driftless,
the only current the wake our weight-shift
slaps into the cove, one oar and not a running
light on the lake, mosquitoes drizzling
from the shallows, the last beer can floating
off the stern, where you threw it at a rainbow
jitterbug snagged in the brush.

SOUNDING HARVEY CREEK

1

Under the narrow, splintering, slatted floor of the dock,
a snake sidles toward the clear shallows,
his head like a dry leaf riding the surface,
his back a string of hourglass bands, hazel and chestnut.
Over the floor of broken shells,
schools of tiny, unseineable minnows dart from his course
and close again as he slides into reeds,
quiver in his wake like slivers of orange light.

I unfold the legs of my chair,
sit and face the water, the mud turtles helmeting snags
and stumps, two mallards skiing into the neck of the creek,
green heads bobbing. Across the pine-bristled back
of Squirrel Island, a heron drags its snaky throat.
Nothing looks more alien to the sky, yellow legs
hanging like sticks. I must seem at least that strange,
my wrist whipping air with a switch of black graphite.

2

I concede my ignorance of fishing,
the stringer coiled
in the bottom of my tackle box, my dull
and virginal Eagle Claws,
my impotent wealth of jitterbugs,
doll flies, Mirr-O-Lures,
spoons that glow like gold jewelry
in their plastic boxes.

What I love about water is mystery,
the something unknowable
curling under roots, the thing lost
sinking deeper

into sludge with each current,
the obscurity of depth
and the infinite variety of oddities
crawling out of that depth
to reveal nothing: frog and stinkpot,
waterdog fanning red gills,
the mole salamander, the common newt,
the dwarf siren, the copperhead
burdening the reeds
with a beautiful danger.

And the hours of awesome ignorance—
enough possibility to make me reel.

3

In the styrofoam bucket, the shiners
fall through my fingers like jewels. Across the wide mouth
of Harvey Creek, nothing stirs in the wooded yards
of retirement homes, the screens still dark in their shades,
the outboards locked in the corners of their boathouses.
Nothing stirs in the black pinetops
feathered with crows.
                    In the reeds behind me
the copperhead waits with the patience of a stick,
and in the middle of the creek
opening into Lake Talquin, the timid water turkeys perch
on the jagged backs of protruding limbs,
motionless above the turtles. I listen for absolute silence
in the unsoundable depth of all water.

A pale bait comes up in my hand and catches light.

Is it wrong not to love the transparency of minnows,
their skeletons showing like veins in a tiny leaf?

IN THE WILDERNESS MOTEL

1

Red star hovering
over the tip of the half-moon, and we follow
the blacktop through fenced and unfenced pasture,
fields of okra
and beans and corn, past
hog farms and shanties, mobile homes scattered
in clusters of shade oak
until we reach the horseshoe drive,
the gravel parking lot
under the burnt-out neon of the Talquin Motel.

Here the weeds have moved in
for good. Rat and coon are regular guests.
Pines root away the concrete walls, drop their limbs
across the roof, and all night
the wind sweeps the rooms,
blows old garbage into different corners.

Where the last reservations are layers of mold
on a plywood desk,
we come to fill a vacancy.

2

Once in Valdosta
the phone rang and we thought we were found out.
It was only a recording, an advertisement
for the Red Fox Lounge,
an extended happy hour with live music.

But that whole evening
we heard voices,
people we knew or thought we knew

singing above the guitar, the electric bass throbbing
up through the floor, through the walls
of our uneasy privacy. And into the night,
their laughter rising like rumors around the pool,
their shadows passing across the pale curtains,
car doors slamming in the parking lot.

3

Around the edge of the dry pool,
beer cans rust in a mulch of needles and leaves,
candy wrappers, paper cups, newspaper
blackened and turning back to pulp. Someone has rocked
the bulbs in the pool lights, splintered
the diving board against the drain. The only music left
is the trees, the wind
cutting high notes over reeds of broken glass.

We sit on a warped deck chair
and watch the cosmic balancing, the red star sliding down
the edge of the moon, the wilderness sliding
across the face of this abandoned motel. Somewhere
in all these wrecked rooms, there is a darkness we can slide
into, a shredded mattress that will ease us into love
and sleep.
　　　　　And when we wake
in the caked layers of leaf-rot, blown-dirt,
burnt-sheet, we can listen through the shattered window
for the raccoon digging in the scattered trash, the grating
of claws on concrete, the owl,
the cicada, the tree frog. We can celebrate
the comfort, the company of ruin.

SLEEPING IN THE JON BOAT

1

Anchored in the middle of hundreds of acres of water,
outboard cut, bait bucket empty and drifting on a stringer,
rod wedged under the cooler and leaning
over the bow, its tip
nodding only at the wind,
the jon boat wallows in the depth, washes around itself
like a twig in an eddy, the slow hand of a watch
losing time.
          Lying in the hull,
across a mattress of flotation cushions, knees crooked
over a seat, head cradled in a rolled towel,
I have only the narrow black punctuated with stars,
the sporadic rally of waves ringing the hull,
the small, hoarse noise of frogs on a far bank,
and crossing the lake, too quick to follow, the gray dart
of an underwing.

2

With the motion of the water becoming the motion of the boat
becoming the motion of the body,
a man could drift away

and find that his sleep has become an entrance into water,
a dream-channel of genes unraveling
like spirals of minnows poured from a bucket,
and the dream
becomes a dream of diving—

an arm hanging over the side of the tilted jon boat,
elbow and forearm dangling
in the warm, green water of Lake Talquin,
thumb and fingers shriveling,

a curling in the joints,
and the white, loose flesh melting together
between the bones.

How deep must the dream go?
The webbed claw?
The fin?

3

Bow-up the jon boat hangs its shadow against the house,
a brick split-level on a corner lot of solid ground
in a suburb of split-levels occupied by men
who sleep and dream of deals and mortgages,
point spreads and golf swings.
                              Over the mouth of my drive
the streetlight flickers like a running light,
and all along the street, the neighborhood has drifted
into the dark, its shallow, clipped lawns flooded
with shadows, dogwoods glazed
like dried scales, azaleas like clotted blood.

I have pushed my chest off the carpet twenty-five times,
brushed and flossed my teeth,
showered, deodorized my underarms. On the night table
a glass of warm beer waits beside a few fishing magazines.
Little else to prolong the inevitable.
                              Why should I dread
the first wave of sleep and wake up fearing my own hand?

IN A PASTURE UNDER A CRADLED MOON

1

Hung between pinetops
three stars cradle the moon. Below, on a sliced hill
where the moss-webs of live oak hang over the roofs
of chicken houses, the chicken wire
of a dog lot leans over the gorge of the new road.
Crouched behind that wire, a dog
barks at the great yellow roundness of the moon.

I listen from this field of stumps,
watch the black cattle
fold their legs, roll full-bellied on the wet ground.
Salt blocks grow around the lip of the pond
like new teeth. Wind combs the ragged Johnson weed,
wrinkles the skin of the water. And I think
how the moonlight falls
or doesn't through the window beyond the field,
the pond, the wall of pines,
falls or doesn't on the bed where you sleep.

2

Who might have been
is like a vague throat-pulse croaking from a cove-shade
or the gargle of bass striking frog spawn, a sound
almost clarifying, like a murmur
from the field's edge, the wing-purr
of horseflies swarming over dung.

Or else like an image
almost solidifying, a cloud of fireflies swarming
between the poplars near the pond, one creature
almost becoming whole, molecular,
but dissolving with the quickness of light.

3

Only a quiet now.
A quiet chorus of frogs, a leg-beat
of crickets, a distant, muffled grinding of a diesel
gearing for a long incline.
And the long black shadows of poplar and pine
streak the field, blossom
with the black hulks of cattle, the charred clusters
of burnt stumps. Between the pinetops
the yellow roundness of the moon
falls through the cup of stars, and I remember how
in the half-hour before sunrise
you cramped and doubled, small blood
spotting the bedsheet, and then a deluge,
the future miscarried.

Wind crackles in the high branches,
rains dry leaves into the field
onto the backs of cattle rolled against the fences.
And in the room where you rest, the ferns
nod from the dresser, the Wandering Jew quivers
from the window basket to the floor, sheet and blanket
curl around your shoulder. I will sit here
only a while longer
studying the way the light drops into the trees,
the way so much love can be learned
from loss.

IN A U-HAUL NORTH OF DAMASCUS

1

Lord, what are the sins
I have tried to leave behind me? The bad checks,
the workless days, the scotch bottles thrown across the fence
and into the woods, the cruelty of silence,
the cruelty of lies, the jealousy,
the indifference?

What are these on the scale of sin
or failure
that they should follow me through the streets of Columbus,
the moon-streaked fields between Benevolence
and Cuthbert where dwarfed cotton sparkles like pearls
on the shoulders of the road. What are these
that they should find me half-lost,
sick and sleepless
behind the wheel of this U-Haul truck parked in a field
   on Georgia 45
a few miles north of Damascus,
some makeshift rest stop for eighteen wheelers
where the long white arms of oaks slap across trailers
and headlights glare all night through a wall of pines?

2

What was I thinking, Lord?
That for once I'd be in the driver's seat, a firm grip
on direction?

So the jon boat muscled up the ramp,
the Johnson outboard, the bent frame of the wrecked Harley
chained for so long to the back fence,
the scarred desk, the bookcases and books,
the mattress and box springs,
a broken turntable, a Pioneer amp, a pair

59

of three-way speakers, everything mine
I intended to keep. Everything else abandon.

But on the road from one state
to another, what is left behind nags back through the distance,
a last word rising to a scream, a salad bowl
shattering against a kitchen cabinet, china barbs
spiking my heel, blood trailed across the cream linoleum
like the bedsheet that morning long ago
just before I watched the future miscarried.

Jesus, could the irony be
that suffering forms a stronger bond than love?

3

Now the sun
streaks the windshield with yellow and orange, heavy beads
of light drawing highways in the dew-cover.
I roll down the window and breathe the pine-air,
the after-scent of rain, and the far-off smell
of asphalt and diesel fumes.

But mostly pine and rain
as though the world really could be clean again.

Somewhere behind me,
miles behind me on a two-lane that streaks across
west Georgia, light is falling
through the windows of my half-empty house.
Lord, why am I thinking about this? And why should I care
so long after everything has fallen
to pain that the woman sleeping there should be sleeping alone?
Could I be just another sinner who needs to be blinded
before he can see? Lord, is it possible to fall
toward grace? Could I be moved
to believe in new beginnings? Could I be moved?

HURRICANE

1

At twilight
the leaves of palmettos screeching like cicadas,
orange limbs rustling around green oranges,
oleanders whining toward the west.
Over the edge of the field,
the pinetops breaking like white water, and the first rain
squalling in from the sea, peppering hollow
on the storm awnings,
washing down the latticed door.

At the church site across the field, animation
and rapture,
lumber scraps rising out of the dirt like Baptists
at the Second Coming. Over the tractor shed
a swirl of shingles, gray wings
beating into the grove, lodging in branches
or rising into the pines across the road.

As long as the gray light holds under the clouds
we stand at the door
and watch how the wind breathes a special life
into everything not tied down.

2

And when the drenched light dies, we sit
in candlelight
and listen to the voice on the radio static,
north-northwest, twelve miles an hour,
and the repeated cautions of fallen wires, bad water,
the deceptive calm of the eye
and the wind that whirls back without warning.

*

What whirls now are shadows
as the candle flickers from the ledge above the cabinet
and the kitchen falls black,
the wind bombing the house with oranges, whistling
under the storm awnings rattling against the walls.

And we wonder if the roof will hold, wonder
until the shot cracks behind us
and a window shatters from a church-stud driven
through an awning, wind exploding the room in glass shrapnel
as we fall from our chairs, in time or not,
to shield our faces from the slivers, to find a door
and close it behind us, give the kitchen up
to the storm.

3

Light gathers
behind a glass door,
and a scrub lizard crawls down the screen.
The oleanders lean back toward the ocean;
bark peeled and strewn,
the melaleuca shakes broken limbs toward the sun.

We cross the grass blown dry in the gales,
walk rows of orange trees and kick the fallen fruit,
piece together a picture of the damage,
a wrecked kitchen, a shed wall collapsed and blown away,
a few lines downed by limbs. Not so much.
Even the half-moon scabbing above my eye
is a good sign, something to be glad for. The way
the quail whistles its reprieve from the saw grass
across the road,
the ox beetle gores up through blown sand.

David Bottoms was born in Canton, Georgia, in 1949. His poems have appeared in many magazines, including *The New Yorker, Atlantic Monthly, Harper's, Poetry, Paris Review,* and *Antaeus,* as well as in numerous anthologies. His first book, *Shooting Rats at the Bibb County Dump,* was chosen by Robert Penn Warren as winner of the 1979 Walt Whitman Award of the Academy of American Poets. He lives with his wife in Atlanta where he teaches creative writing at Georgia State University.